FREDDY THE FROG
AND THE PRINCESS

For Alona, whose kisses can do that and more.

Published by
Baby Matters Inc.

515 West 29th Street, New York NY 10001, U.S.A.
tel 212 242 7123 • fax 212 366 9739 • E-mail ari@inch.com

©1998 Zygmunt Frankel, all rights reserved • (P)1998 Baby Matters Inc.
First edition: January 1998 • Printed In Hong Kong

Library Of Congress Catalog Card Number: 97-93971
ISBN: 1-888509-08-2

Freddy The Frog on the internet: www.inch.com/~ari/freddy.html

FREDDY THE FROG
AND THE PRINCESS

by
Zygmunt Frankel

baby matters

One beautiful morning,
Freddy the Frog sat on the
bank of his little pond in the
woods, listening to the birds
and enjoying life in general.

Among the trees appeared a young princess.

The princess caught Freddy the Frog,

gave him a kiss,

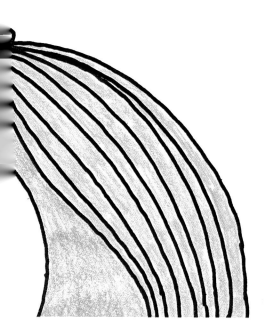

and Freddy turned into a prince!

"Wonderful!" said the princess. "The witch was right! If you kiss a frog, he might turn into a prince! Now we shall get married and live happily ever after!"

Freddy was rather confused by what had happened to him. What's more, he was not sure you have to marry the first princess who kisses you.

"Just a moment," said the princess. "Where's your white horse and shining armor?"

"Never had any," said Freddy.

"And you have big feet."

"Always had them."

"Well, never mind," said the princess. "Let's go and show you to the witch."

In the middle of the forest stood the witch's hut.

The princess introduced
Freddy to the witch and
thanked her for her advice.

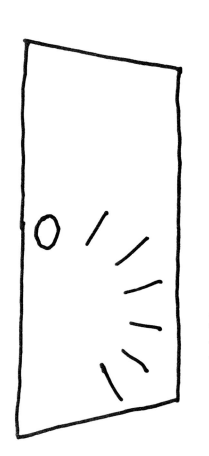

Suddenly there came a
low knock on the door

There stood Freddy's best friends: Dwarf, Field Mouse and two little twin fish whom Dwarf carried in a bucket.

"Excuse us," said Dwarf. "Have you by any chance seen our friend Freddy the Frog? We've been looking for him since this morning but he seems to have disappeared. His friends the two little twin fish also wanted to join, so we took them along in a bucket."

"Friends, it's me!" said Freddy.
"I've turned into a man!"

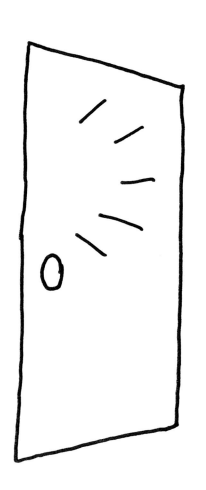

There came another
knock on the door.

It was a young prince
in shining armor,
leading a white horse.

"Excuse me," said the
prince. "Is there a
young princess around
here by any chance?"

Now the princess had a problem.
"Could I marry both of them?" she asked.

"Better not," said the witch.
"It causes all sorts of trouble,
and it's also against the law."

"I have an idea," said Freddy.
"Could I turn back into a frog?"

"I could try," said the witch.

The prince and the princess
rode off to get married,

and they invited Freddy and all his friends to the wedding, as special guests of honor.

THE END